*For Mom and Dad*
~J.S.

*For Jodie*
~C.W.

First published in the United States 1996 by
Little Tiger Press,
12221 West Feerick Street, Wauwatosa, WI 53222-2117
Originally published in Great Britain 1996 by
Magi Publications, London
Text © 1996 Julie Sykes
Illustrations © 1996 Catherine Walters
CIP Data is available.
All rights reserved.
Reprinted by arrangement with Little Tiger Press.
Printed in U.S.A.

1 3 5 7 9 10 8 6 4 2

# Sara Squirrel
## and the
# Lost Acorns

*by* Julie Sykes

*Pictures by* Catherine Walters

On the edge of Teasel Wood in a large tree
lived Sara Squirrel. Like most squirrels,
she was always hungry.
One day, when Sara visited her secret store
for an acorn snack, she found it empty.

"Oh dear, I don't remember eating *everything*,"
said Sara peering into all the corners, just in case
she'd missed something. "Well, I guess I'll have
to go out and gather more acorns."

Sara scampered down the tree trunk and along the forest path toward the oak trees deep in the woods.

On the way she met Merry Mouse.

"Sara! I'm so glad to see you!" she cried. "Are you going into the woods? The babies are keeping me so busy I haven't had time to find dinner. Would you bring me back a juicy berry?"

Sara liked to help her friends, so she cheerfully agreed. Off she went, saying to herself, "A juicy berry and acorns for me."

Sara hadn't gone much farther when she heard
another voice.

"Who's there?" asked Morris Mole, poking his
head out of his molehill.

"It's me!" shouted Sara loudly, before she
remembered that Morris was nearsighted, not deaf.

"If you're going into the woods, will you bring me
back a crunchy leaf?" asked Morris politely.
"They're so much better than the ones I find here."
"All right, I will," said Sara in a quieter voice.
She hurried on, chanting, "A crunchy leaf, a juicy
berry and acorns for me."

"Who's making that noise?" said Barney Badger gruffly as he climbed out of his burrow. "Oh, it's you, Sara. Are you going into the woods?"

"Yes I am," said Sara. "Can I get you anything?"

"Well, since you ask, I'd like a mushroom – and make sure it's a tasty one."

"A tasty mushroom," Sara repeated, "a crunchy leaf, a juicy berry and acorns for me."

Soon Sara reached the oak trees.
"Lots of acorns," she thought happily,
gathering them up. "Plenty for my store,
and one for a snack."

Next Sara found a mushroom. "Tasty!" she said, sampling a piece from its cap.

She balanced the mushroom on top of the acorns, and off she went.

A little farther on, Sara discovered a bright
red berry and a crunchy leaf. She put them
on top of the mushroom.

Staggering along with her goodies, she didn't
see the snail in her path, and . . .

. . . down fell Sara,
the acorns,
the tasty mushroom,
the crunchy leaf and
the juicy berry.
"Bother!" she said, gathering
everything up again. She was
really hungry now, and couldn't
wait to get home.

When she arrived, Merry, Morris and Barney were
waiting for her.

"We thought you'd never come," barked Barney,
eyeing the tasty mushroom.

"Thank you, Sara," said Morris, thrilled with
his crunchy leaf.

"I'll share this with my babies," squeaked Merry,
rushing away with the juicy berry.

Suddenly Sara remembered her own snack.
"Where are *my* acorns?" she cried, looking
around. They were nowhere to be seen.

Poor Sara! She was so loaded down with food
for everyone else, she'd lost her acorns.
"Well, I'll have to go back and get some more,"
she sighed.

As Sara set out for the oak trees for the second
time that day, a cheery voice called her name.
"Sara, since you're going out, could you bring
me back a seed?" It was Victoria Vole.

"Oh no, not again," Sara thought, and before
Victoria could say anything else she ran off,
pretending not to hear her.
"Poor Sara," said Victoria to herself. "I do
believe she's going deaf."